GRUESOME TALES FROM A BROKEN MIND 2

A Short Story Anthology

BEREK MORRIS

Berek Morris
Gruesome Tales From a Broken Mind 2
Silkhaven Publishing, LLC
Smashwords Edition

Join Berek Morris' mailing list for games, freebies, and fun at http://www.berekmorris.com/newsletter

Please visit author Berek Morris on his website http://www.berekmorris.com

Berek Morris enjoys connecting with fans on social media. Please find him at:
Facebook: @AuthorBerekMorris

This anthology is his second collection of psychological thriller flash-fiction stories.

CONTENTS

Silkhaven Publishing, LLC

ISBN: 978-1-948997-36-2 (mobi)

ISBN: – 978-1-948997-37-9 (epub)

ISBN: 978-1-948997-38-6 (paperback)

Library of Congress Control Number:

(V1) – Dec 15, 2019

DISCAIMERS:

This novel is for mature audiences only. Violence, sex, and/or nudity are described in this book and the target audience is for individuals 18+ years of age.

A KING IN AN EMPTY CASTLE

Dying candles lightly dust a large empty throne room with a small glimmer of light. Tables stretch out covered with gorgeous but empty china plates laying atop the fanciest tablecloths man can own. Hundreds of empty, pure silver wine glasses are poised eloquently with refined silverware perched ever so lightly upon elegant silk napkins. A long red carpet with gold trim is in the center of the room, leading up three steps to lay at the foot of a large throne made of gold.

Upon that throne sits a man, not an ordinary man but a king dressed in the most beautiful clothing money can buy, only for it to be thrown in a closet one day, never to see the light of day again. The king is draped back into his throne, one leg extended, the other supporting him up as he rests his chin in his palm. An expression of bore and sorrow preside on his face. After a dull silence, a small murmur breaks the emptiness. It is from the king.

"Here I sit for another night. In an empty room full of nothing but past memories. A million glasses and plates but not one person to use them. Thousands of wine bottles from the vineyard and yet no one to drink them. The rarest meats and spices from around the land, and yet I can't even find a single man to partake in the feast." The king sits in silence for what feels like hours. His expression doesn't change.

"In front of me lies everything a person can dream of, riches, food, drink, no reason ever to lift a finger, and yet here I sit, surrounded by empty walls and an even emptier hall." Slowly the king starts to rise up, using the arms of the chair to support his shifting weight. The king is an old man with white hair and wrinkles hidden behind an unkempt, long, dirty beard. His frail body shakes as he moves. The sparkle one has in their eye has faded from his, and what is left is just a hollow shell diving into an even hollower soul. After the king has situated himself right, he inspects the room. His expression grows brighter.

"To think the celebration after the sea beast's death was held here. How the champion fishermen were treated as heroes from that night forward.

There was also the night my cousin was announced as head Duke of his family, and the village that comes with it. This is the same hall that my sister was asked for her hand in marriage. The hall even honored the first man I knighted be sitting right in front of where I stand. The special night that my younger brother had found his love was the same that we found out about my older brother's firstborn child was to be attending us within nine months." The king's face starts to shift from the slightest ray of happiness to a hollowed-out shell again. "The same place where we held one last night of remembrance for my brother who died in combat. That same night when we all found out the betrayal of our closest so-called friends. The same night where my royal family was poisoned. The same night where I watched everyone die and held my wife for one last time." The king's expression returns to sorrow as he begins to walk back over to his throne and after a few struggles, manages to sit back in the same position just a few minutes ago.

More time passes as the king sits in his throne, making not even the faintest sound despite his mind going a thousand miles a minute. Finally, the king stirs in his seat. Without changing the expression on his face, he reaches into his robe pocket and pulls out a small vial with skull and crossbones. The vial contains a black thick liquid and reeks like eggshells and sewage. The king palms it over and over again in his hand, turning it over on each side, scrutinizing it, never taking his eyes off of it. Finally, after some careful consideration, he decides to uncork the vial, letting out the aroma of death to sweep over his senses.

The king lets out a long and exasperated sigh before he slowly brings it up to his lips. As he gradually turns the vial onto its side, anticipating the flowing sensation of drinking something, he stops himself right before any dripped out. The king pulls the vial back down and stares at the label again. Thoughts begin to ponder their way back into his head.

"Would it even make a difference if I drank it?"

GLARING EYES

All I want is peace. Peace, from the stares. Everywhere I go, they watch me. See me, right through me even. I go grocery shopping, and they know. I go for a walk, and they know. I leave my house, and they are there, waiting. I can't get a moment of my own without them around. Everywhere, all the time, they can see that I am–just some freak and monster. Almost as if I ooze vileness, they can detect it. Try my best, but you can't hide what's on the inside. Just some large monster.

I don't want to be. I just want to live my life and have minimal interaction. I just want to go out and enjoy what little joy I have left, but I am not allowed this pleasure. Never will I be truly alone. Like some ogre in a sea of royalty, they know that I am there. They don't even hide their stares sometimes.

I didn't want this. If it were me, I would find some cave and wither away, never to be remembered, as insignificant as some fly.

I see the stares, the looks. I see the horror and anger in their eyes when they see me. The fake smiles they put on when they must interact with me. The way they wipe their hands and scurry away to safety with their kind when they are done talking to me. I'm just tired of being seen as a monster...

THE SMELL OF FEAR

My heart is racing. I'm breathing heavy. Sweat barrels down my forehead, my body trembling as I lay here, trying to hide behind an old log. Fear flows through my pores, rushing around inside me until it envelopes my being and essence. My thoughts are stammered and hard to focus on anything other than, "what was that thing."

The night is quiet. No wind, no twigs snapping, no leaves falling, just my heart racing inside my chest. I dare not move a muscle. I lay as still as I can, trying to hear whatever that beast is. It is huge and fast. It leaps from tree to tree using its paws alone. It lets out a cry that makes us stop dead in our tracks. That is our first mistake.

"Where is that thing?" I ask myself. After what feels like ages, finally, I decide to slightly adjust my body. Slowly, I raise my head to the sky above me. Drool slaps my cheek, for I am met with rows upon rows of sharp dagger-like teeth. A snarl erupts from the jaws of this creature.

My scream doesn't ever finish...

4

LESS THAN A FLY ON THE WALL

Alone I walk this forsaken planet. Alone I live day to day, surrounded by nothing but the pain and hatred I give myself. I walk past thousands of wandering souls; little do they know that a husk walks with them. Where do you go when the pleasures in life turn on you?

When the night creeps, its eerie shadow lurks through the windows, letting in all of the dark that the sun promised to take away. Restless, I lay awake thinking, nay, dreaming of a different life, but not dreaming of changing it.

For all of the wishes and hopes and desires that this world creates and shows, the one that I wish for is impossible to achieve.

I wish to be nothing more than a fly on the wall. Trading everything for the life of something that doesn't matter. To slip away, never to be seen again or cared for, the pain that occurs from my existence is worth a trade for a meaningless life. All of the sorrow and memories that keep you at night, that keeps the tears rolling down your cheeks, that makes you toss and turn, the constant anger and fear, all gone, forever, with but one simple wish.

To poof into thin air, unseen, unheard of, never to be remembered, and no memories to recall. Essentially to never have even existed at all. Never to be anything more than a fly on the wall.

Such a shame that suicide is easier.

BLOODY ROUTINE

Every day you wake up. Every day you get out of bed with hesitation, regretting the previous night's decision, and every morning we get up and do the same routine.

We all have our breakfast rituals, getting dressed in clothes you have had forever, brushing your teeth and combing your hair. Putting in the effort to make yourself seem presentable only for you to hate every part of it.

You begrudgingly get to school or work where you sit and do tasks and do labor that seem to never end. You struggle to make it to lunch, where the same food options day in and day out are available. And then lunch break is never long enough. You watch the clock go down, knowing that this won't make lunch any longer. As the metaphorical bell rings, you pack up your things, and the frown grows stronger on your face. The day finally ends, and while you feel happy, it doesn't last long and is only situational. Once your home from your day, you throw off the clothes that restrained your mere moments ago only to find yourself still bored but now in your underwear. Maybe tonight you'll make another microwave meal, watch reruns of shows that you have seen scores of times before, finish off another bottle of whatever is in stock, and wait for the last few hours of the day to end so that tiredness can whisk you away from your sleep.

Oh, but don't worry... you get to do it all again tomorrow...

❧ 6 ❧

THE DEVIL'S DEAL

The command is ordered. As the king's sword lifts towards the gate, a barrage of artillery lands on the heavy wooden doors, breaking them to rubble. The king dismounts, and the other lieutenants and I follow. Weapons in hand, shields are drawn and at the ready, we start our march inside the castle.

The hallway is long and dark, mysterious as it is eerie. With baby steps, we hesitate to move onwards. We look towards our king for guidance. The look of determination doesn't leave his face for a moment. "FEAR DID NOT BRING US THIS FAR; FEAR WILL NOT STOP US NOW!" He bellows at us. Despite it being a few words, it was more than enough to rally us again. Onwards, we approached the throne room...

Fire illuminates the room, revealing a black and bleak burnt cobblestone wall and floor. A long purple carpet suggesting its attention to a throne made of bones. Upon that throne sits the king of hell himself, leaned back and with a grin. Beside him stands a tall brute, covered in ripped muscles and titanium armor, as well as a haggard old woman in a hooded cloak. Lucifer's generals.

"Ah, dear King, so glad you were able to make it. The guards didn't give you too much trouble, did they?" His grin never leaves his face.

"Lucifer! You have plagued my lands and tormented my people long enough! On this day, you will face redemption for your actions!"

Lucifer adjusts his posture, leaning forward in his throne. "Say, your Highness, that is quite the army you have brought. Must have taken you months to assemble and rally all these soldiers. What's even more impressive, is the EASE it took for you to get to me. Surely you must have thought your numbers heavy to accomplish this job?" Lucifer ends that question on a high note. I turn to face my king, to see the expression of a leader on his face turned to one of confusion.

"Seems like your still not understanding, king. Let me explain." As Lucifer finishes the statement, a large rectangular mirror behind him transforms itself into a viewing portal. Through the portal lays hundreds of thousands of undead troops overlooking various towns and villages.

"You see, while you were gathering your army to come to lay siege upon my kingdom, I was doing the same thing. In the months that have led to this very moment, you have gone from village to village, town to town, gathering everyone and anyone who can hold a weapon and march by your side. While you were doing that, I was doing the same. I was summoning troops and raising your fallen to have them hide and wait. Waiting for the day you were ready. For the day that mankind would charge up my mountain, knock down my walls, and burst in on me gung-ho. Well, your Highness, you have. Now what happens next is up to you. We can clash swords here, I barely break a sweat as my generals and remaining troops rip you to shreds, all the while these forces in hiding raise hell to your kingdom. If you somehow win this fight, by the time you return home, there will be nothing but ash and dust along with a hungry, undead army. Or..."

Lucifer extends his arm; he is holding a large parchment and pen. He then sets it out on a table in front of him.

"You sign this here deal."

The rest of the lieutenants are speechless, all

staring at their king. No sound is made. The King stares wide-eyed at the portal, every second dragging him down as the numbers of the enemy armies seem to be endless. The king's mouth opens slightly in shock as the situation laid out in front of him starts to set in his mind. Finally, the king speaks.

"What.... what is the deal?"

THE SOUND OF FREEDOM

I hear chanting. Loud and in unison. They are not speaking English. My eyes are blindfolded with a thick cloth. My hands are bound behind me. My mouth is blocked. I am on my knees, lost to the world around me. The only sense I have is hearing, and all I have to listen to is the same few words being chanted. "Sanquis enim Infigens."

The chanting continues for what feels like ages. Panic has had time to set in, set up shop, and leave. Suddenly a voice emerges through the chanting.

"BROTHERS IN BLOOD," it shouts. "TONIGHT IS THE NIGHT OF THE GREAT AWAKENING! THESE SACRIFICES WILL BRING FORTH EVERYTHING WE HAVE BEEN PROMISED AND MORE!"

The crowd erupts into joyous cheers and

applause. It sounded like hundreds of people are there, lavishing the moment.

"BRING FORTH THE CEREMONIAL KNIFE!" the same voice yelled. The chanting resumes, this time steadily getting louder and quicker. An Arm grabs me and pulls me to my feet. Panic resets within me.

Forcefully, I am taken up some steps and thrown back to my knees on some wood platform. The voice from earlier sounds much closer now. It starts to speak in a language I cannot understand. The crowd is eating every word and moment of it. The voice yells again in English. "FOR THE FINAL INGRE-DIENT, ONE PINT OF HUMAN BLOoo...". The voice trails off. It is followed by a multitude of thuds and metal clanging, collapsing to the ground below them. The world is silent. No noise, no chanting, no forceful movement, just utter silence. Confusion strikes me. What is happening now?

A voice enters my mind, a voice that is not my own. It hits me like a cold wind, sending shivers up and down my spine. "You...are...welcome..." the voice says. My hands are suddenly unbound. In a flash, I remove the rest of the binds that restrict me. I take off the blindfold. I look around where I am. I am on a wooden platform, surrounded by trees and nature. A torch illuminates the platform. Beyond that, I see something that sends terror into my body.

Around me lays dozens of bodies, all non-responsive and dead. They each are in purple robes; some have metallic weapons strewn about them. However, no blood rests anywhere. I look around to see if my rescuer is nearby, but I am alone. I am completely alone, surrounded by death.

❋ 8 ❋

SOUL STEALER

Insomnia strikes me again tonight. No matter what I try, I can't fall asleep. It's 2:58 in the morning, and I'm stuck staring at the clock. Drawn in by the face, waiting and watching the seconds slowly and steadily go by. It is as boring as it sounds.

As I start to get lost staring at the clock, mesmerized by the pace of it, it suddenly stalls. The clock stops precisely one second before 3AM. I blink, and my consciousness comes back to me. I rub my eyes and start to slowly rise to get some new batteries. I stumble in the dark but manage to find my way to the drawer with batteries, but when I return, the clock is working just fine. I check my watch. The clock's time is correct. I glance at my desktop and see that it confirms the same as the watch. I stand confused and dazed. Surely, I didn't imagine that, but what else could it be? After a few more seconds of trying to figure it out, I go back to the process. I lay down on my bed and stare at the clock on the wall, just watching the seconds go by. At some point, I finally drift off.

The next night I am stricken again with misfortune, and I am restless with insomnia. Tonight, however, a change of scenery. I'm sitting on my balcony, watching the cloudless and peaceful night sky with dancing stars. Every now and then I'll see a car pass on the road. They are few and far between, but still just enough to be a constant reminder that I am not alone. One truck, in particular, grabs my attention. It is loud and large. A monstrosity with four wheels in the back. It flies down the road, darting between lanes, sporadically moving back and forth, and then it comes to a halt. No brakes, no momentum, just entirely still. I look over at the truck. There is no reason for it to have stopped. I realize that the world is following the truck. There is no movement or sounds at all. My mind is bewildered by the sudden drop in activity. I look at my watch. 2:59, one second before 3am, and completely stopped. My gaze darts to the truck. Something is there.

Something that sends goosebumps up and down my spine.

A large hovering specter-like creature mounts the truck. A finely defined beam of light erupts from the driver's side of the truck. Mimicking a moth to light, the beam swiftly charges at the creature, being absorbed into the creature's skin. I am frozen with curiosity and shock. What is happening? What is this beast? What is it doing?!

Before my mind can start to formulate answers, the world starts up again, and the creature vanishes with a fine mist. As the world resets, the truck moves again. The swerving continues, but no longer between traffic lanes and this time straight into a tree. At full force, the monstrous truck slams its front into what might as well have been a thick wall. The truck folds into itself, smashing it beyond hope of repair, the windshield is broken into hundreds of sharp shards, the driver, half in the vehicle and the half sprayed over the hood. In a word, massacred. My eyes will not do anything else but be glued wide open, jaw agape, mind racing for any meaning of how what, and why. Without a doubt, the driver is dead, and whatever that thing was killed him.

Unlike the night before, I do not sleep a wink.

The next day is dreadful. The headline for the

news that day read, "Drunk Driver Meets an Early End!" Without reading anything, I know exactly who they mean. I don't tell anyone what I saw, who would believe me? Hell, I barely believe myself. The rest of the day goes by in a blur, almost as if time itself was faster than usual. Before I even realize, it's 2:58 am again.

I find myself once again on the balcony, staring off into the world around me. I am counting down the seconds. Just 20 seconds remaining. What will happen tonight? What is that creature? 12 seconds remaining. Who was that person in the truck? 8 seconds remaining. Will it show up tonight? Will it attack someone again? 1 second remaining. 2:59, and my watch stops exactly a second before 3 o'clock hits. I look up to the now frozen world. Once again, nothing is a stir.

Seconds turn into minutes. Nothing is happening. I keep checking my watch, but it is still stopped. I lean over the railing, squint my eyes, and cup my hands, trying to see if the creature is just out of sight. More time passes. Maybe the creature isn't here tonight. As I reach for my chair to take a seat, fear flows into my body. Whatever I just grabbed, wasn't my chair.

My head and body slowly start to shift towards

whatever I am touching. My hand feels cold as if I was grabbing onto and holding ice packs. As I stare at it, it stares back at me. Next to me sits a broad specter like creature, and in my hand, I hold one of its many arms. An arm pieced together by rotting flesh and bone, strung up with stitches, sewn together like a cheap dress. The specter is three times my size, towering over me, staring right into my being with red glowing eyes. It has no other facial features; the many arms stick out from under a black cloth that covers most of it. Cold seeps from under the creature, a smoky mist that escapes from the bottom of the cloth.

I try to let go of its arm, but I can't. I try to take a step back, but my feet and legs resist. I try to say something, but my lips will not open. I can't move my head or body. I am completely frozen in place. I can't even shift my eyes from the creature. Without any kind of a mouth, it begins to speak.

As if it were my own thoughts, I hear what the creature says. "Lifeforce, plentiful. Soul, untouched. Threat level, minimum. Consumption, imminent." I lose all feeling in my body except for ache and strain. The feeling of vomiting, a day after working out intensely, giving blood, and every known sickness hit me, and every second, it gets worse.

First, my arms drop down to my side, too weak to

hold themselves. My Back and knees give out. My vision goes blurry. Memories, like my mind, go blank. My breathing and my heart rate drop. I'm gasping for air, eyes are twitching with panic, sweat leaves my body, tears roll down my face, and then everything comes to an end.

THE INTERNAL HUNGER

I am always hungry. Nothing satisfies my appetite. I feast all day on every kind of food, but nothing fills me. I am always thirsty. Nothing quenches my thirst. My fridge is stocked to the brim with all sorts of delicious goods, but it means nothing to me, for the taste of it all is meaningless.

I crave for something else, for something different. The meat isn't filling, and the booze never gets me drunk. More and more, I find myself refusing to eat. What's the point?

Every day I grow thinner and thinner, wasting away to nothing, yet my fridge stays stocked. My pantry is full of canned goods and non-perishables; my cupboard is filled with bread and spices. A full kitchen stocked with enough to feed a kingdom for years, and I don't even want a crumb.

I don't crave food anymore; I don't lust for companionship or romance. I'm constantly drained and bored with the day-to-day of the dullness that is a routine life. I crave for something else, something more fun, something... weak.

I'm starving for some weak-minded prey. I toss and turn at night, dreaming of claiming another victim, someone to slowly torture and corrupt until they end up scared and feeling alone. Every waking moment is kept with the thought of the pleasure to feast upon just one more mind.

It's all like a little game to me, the meeting of someone new, someone who doesn't know of me. Then I slowly install fear and paranoia into their easily influenced mind. Tricking them into believing their friends don't love them. Making them see what they believe to be the truth when, in reality, I block reality with smoke and mirrors, forcing them to rely on me to keep granting them the so-called "truth."

They follow me and plead to stay as I rot their sanity to the core. That's when they are ready. After I destroy what little sanity they have left, I leave them, letting them realize the horror of their actions, the pain, and suffering that they have dispensed to their once so-called friends and family. I leave them like a husk of their former selves, and then when they come crawling back to me, begging for forgiveness and crying for me to come back, I know I have won.

That's when the feast begins. That's when I offer them the only way to feel better, the only way to feel good about their miserable little life, the one cure-all for them. A swift and painless death. And once they do it, I revel in the moment for no longer am I hungry and thirsty. Finally, I am full. And once I'm done feasting on this broken mind, I move on to my next meal...

❧ 10 ❧

A FRIENDS LAST REQUEST

A knock at my door grabs my attention. I go to answer it, and to my surprise, my friend is standing there with a box of their belongings. He looks like he's been crying, yet he has a smile on his face. "Hey, sorry about just dropping by, but I just wanted to give you some stuff," as he talks, he gestures towards my house, implying we should talk inside.

"Uh, yeah, come on in." I get out of the way and open my door wider. He nods his head and enters my house.

He sets his stuff down and hands me an envelope. "You're my best friend, and I can tell you anything right?" He asks with a loaded question tone.

"Of course, what's up?" I respond.

He lets out a long sigh. "I've made up mind on

how I want to live life, and I've decided I don't. I'm done. In this box is everything I want you to have." He slaps the box lightly.

I'm speechless. I think to myself, perhaps I must have misheard him. I stare at him, waiting for the joke, the punchline or something, but it never comes.

After a few seconds, words finally come to my mouth. "What...what do you mean, you don't?"

He looks me directly in the eye and takes a moment before he responds. "I mean, I'm going to kill myself." The room is silent for a moment before he begins talking again.

"Now before you get all emotional and mushy, I've been to therapists, counselors, teachers, anyone and everyone with an ear, and they all say the same thing. "I understand, try to think more positive, there is always tomorrow. I've taken and been on countless drugs, prescribed and not prescribed, and all they do is fuck with me, and honestly, I'm done."

He says all of this with a smile. I have nothing to reply to this bombshell. He can see my expression of shock and confusion and goes in for a hug. As he hugs me, he says something under his breath so quiet that if he weren't this close, I wouldn't hear him. "You're my best friend, close enough to be family. I know this is sudden and weird, but this is my decision, and I thank you for supporting me. I just wanted to say goodbye."

He pulls back from the hug. Tears are rolling down my eyes, I'm trying to say something, but he looks so determined and happy. For the first time in a long time, I see something in him.

He starts to leave, and as he gets to the door, he turns back and says the last thing he'll ever say to me. "It's been fun, hopefully, one day, in another life or place, we can hang out again."

PULLING AN EMPTY TRIGGER

My lips slide over the barrel as the shotgun fits nicely on my tongue. My tongue tastes the metal. Next to me a handwritten note, In it is written my apology to the world, all of the things that drove me here, all the things I did, all the things I didn't, all of the reasons as to why I'm here, and finally my last goodbye to this cruel and miserable world.

I pray that the next place I go to is better. A lone tear starts to roll down my face. Finally, I arrive at the end of this miserable ride. I let out my last breath as I push on the trigger.

Click

My heart stops. I look down, wondering if it worked. I assumed it would be louder. I opened my eyes slowly and one at a time. I see no blood or any sign of a mess. Did it work?

Slowly the realization sets in. The gun wasn't loaded. Nothing happened. I drop the shotgun. It topples down to my feet. I slam my head into my shaky hands. Tears start to flow like a river down my arms.

I don't know what's worse, the fact that I just had a gun to my head from my own doing, or the fact that I regret not loading ammo.

WHAT STOPS YOU?

What stops you?

When the voices start to chime in, what stops you?

When all you can think about is the pain of it all, what stops you?

When all you can think about is the suffering and the bleak, what stops you?

When all you can do is sit and cry, when all you want is for the pain to go away, when all you can do is sit and think about the past and the present, all of the things you regret and all of the things that keep you up at night, what stops you from ending it all?

I'm still trying to find my reason. Hopefully, I find it soon...

ALWAYS CHECK THE BLINDS

God DAMN do I hate it when they struggle. Always makes me sweaty and out of breath. Using the back of my hand, I wipe the sweat from my brow, flicking off the left-over droplets. I get off of the woman below me. Up until recently, I owed her a hundred dollars. Now she is just some dead hooker. Barely clothed, she lays sprawled on the bed on her back, her throat heavily bruised and swollen with hand marks. A black eye begins to set in as well. She looks so still, almost like a life-size doll.

I reach into my bag and pull out a bone saw. I put on my mask and goggles and drag the body to the floor. With a decent thud, the body does as I direct. I crack my knuckles and my neck, adorn my usual twisted smile, and forcefully grind the bone saw into the bodies shoulder. I am met with a gasp.

In shock, I turn to the woman. However, she has made no change in her amount of life. My brow burrows lower into my eyes, surely, I was not mistaken. I could have sworn I heard someone gasp...

As my thought almost finishes, I hear a bump from the hallway outside. Hastily, I swing my head towards the window. I make eye contact with a little boy through the window. His eyes are wide, and his mouth is agape in horror. Mere seconds after our eyes lock, I see him shift over and start fleeing down the walkway. Almost like instinct, I begin to chase. As I reach the door, A single thought enters my mind.

"This one surely is going to throw the detectives in a loop..."

❧ 14 ❧

THE HUNTER AWAKENS

It's dark out tonight. Complete silence in the air. A slight wind blows, letting in all sorts of aromas into my nose, filling my senses with the knowledge that prey is out tonight. My crooked smile forms from ear to ear. Soon I will kill again.

My legs strain themselves down, crouching, bending to get my body as low to the ground as possible. Slowly, I crawl against the floor. I don't make a sound.

I wait patiently. I know there is prey out there. I can smell their fear. I love the smell of it. It's a mixture of sweat and dirt, but for some reason, it makes a sweet scent, like freshly poured honey. The smell is getting stronger. My next kill is nearby.

I wait patiently, letting my ears pick up on the smallest twig snap and lightest bristle of a bush. It's heading east of me. Slowly I creep forward. I don't think it hears me. I love it when it doesn't hear its upcoming death. The surprise makes it better.

I get into a good ambush spot and lay as low to the ground as possible. I can hear it walking towards me. It has no idea. Each step slightly louder than the last, each step making my grin bigger and bigger. Soon I will have another kill.

Just five more steps, and it will be all over. Four... Three... Two... One... GOTCHA!

I lunge out from my hiding spot and jab my blade into the victim's chest. Twisting the blade, I see her eyes fade from pain to nothing as her soul leaves her body. She falls to the ground, lifeless.

I get a good look at my victim. She's nothing more than a child, ten years at most. Her flowery dress now soaked in her own blood. I look around me to see that no one had seen us.

Good, I'd rather not have to deal with any witnesses. I look back at the body, more blood has been soaked into the dress. I take out a small flower and place it on her forehead. Just a small calling card to keep the detectives busy. I adjust my posture and start to leave the scene. As I leave the park, a thought enters my mind. Never let your children walk home alone once the moon rises.

15

SOMEONE ELSE'S DARK DUNGEON

My eyes burst open as I awaken to hear blood-curdling screams coming from somewhere. The room must be pitch black because I can't see more than a couple feet in front of me. The screams are close, and they aren't dying down. I try to move my arms, but they refuse to budge. Instead, I am met with the sound of chains clashing together. I get the same response from my feet.

The screams continue. This time they get cut off mid yell. Now they are being held back by the sound of gurgling. It sounds like someone threw a bucket of water on the floor. Someone starts to curse out loud, praying and blasphemy to God. Whatever they are saying, I can tell no one from up above is listening to their pleas.

Just as quick as the screaming started, it ends. No more screams, no more cursing, and no more pleas. Silence descends upon me. The screams were somehow more comforting.

Time passes at an unrecognizable pace. Minutes feel like hours, and hours feel like minutes. No sound ever comes. I'm left alone with my own thoughts. What's happening? Where am I? Who was screaming? More time passes.

A sharp creaking sound breaks the barrier. It sounds like an old wooden door opening. I can barely make out what is in front of me. A small sliver of light from a match adds little to the amount of light in the room, and mostly just adds shadows. However, it is just enough to get an outline of what's in front of me. A large, humanoid creature, with a slim body and bulging muscles, starts to slowly walk into the room. As it gets closer to me, I hear a voice in my head, not one of my own.

"...scream...it only makes it better..."

As the voice starts to leave, the figure in front of me starts to encroach towards me revealing another set of arms with long sharp blades on each, its mouth opens up to show rows of sharp teeth, blood dripping off of them. My mind snaps. I let out every scream I have ever had in me, I'm begging and praying for whatever it is to leave. My screams get interrupted as two sharp claws thrust into my stomach. My head feels light. I spit out blood upon the floor. It's first set of arms reach out and grab my shoulders as its open mouth gets inches from my face.

Before his teeth chomp down, the same voice from earlier re-enters my mind. "...scream...scream all you want...it only makes it better..."

16

FORCED RESURRECTION

Air is shoved into my lungs, my body aches to life as I reopen my eyes. Pain shoots throughout my entire being as my limbs struggle to remember the way they are supposed to act. My eyes dart around my surroundings. I am in some sort of dark and damp place with mere candle-light to light the room.

I try to move my arm out and raise myself up, but the leather restraint stops me. Startled, I look down at myself. I am on some table, naked, and tied down like some experiment. My skin is rotting away, bones stick out of me, and I am riddled with holes and scars. My movements are slow.

Through the silence, a voice emerges. It is some old man with a voice as cracked as he is wrinkly. His cloak hides most of his body, excluding his face and hands. He slowly wanders over to me until he is hovering next to me. I feel woozy, out of it. If I were drugged, I am still under the effects.

The man's hand reaches out and grabs me by my chin. He keeps tossing and turning my head, murmuring to himself.

"...response is low... eyes bloodshot... that arm is useless... lower jaw broken...". He trails off in his thoughts. He then walks over to a small fire pit and pulls out a metal rod with the tip glowing bright red. Without saying a thing, he walks over to me and jabs the rod into my shoulder. The pain is non-existent. Confused I stare at the man. He looks back at me, dead in my eyes.

"This zombie is ready for the meat grinder..."

17

CHANGE IN A SECOND

Smoke pours out of the barrel as the flash of the bullet starts to fade. I open my eyes. The shakiness in my hands dies down as the gun nuzzles itself against my palm.

My breath starts to settle itself after a few seconds. My heartbeat slowly returns to normal. The world seems silent and quiet now as if everything else took a few seconds to just breath, but all things must come to an end.

As the man, now with a bullet hole in his chest, collapses to the ground holding his wound with the hand not clenching the knife, a thud reignites the sounds of the world. Cars start to honk in the street, loud, drunk chicks begin to scream at each other with laughter, homeless continue to ask for change as those better off ignore them.

I tuck the gun back into the holster and take a look around me. Some dirty back alley, dripping with grim and sludge, and now another dead mugger falls upon its floor. I wonder if he ever had the thought that this is how he would go? Some no-named mugger in some no-named back alley.

18

HAIKU: LIFE AND DEATH

L ife is short-lived
      Full of misery and pain
      Life seems to never end (Life seems so
endless)5 syllables

D eath suits everyone
      For it is an ugly truth
      And truth rarely hurts

I hope you enjoyed reading this collection. Please leave a review:

https://authorberekmorris.wordpress.com/ GTFABM2-info/

Interested in reading the first collection, 'Gruesome Tales from a Broken Mind'?

https://authorberekmorris.wordpress.com/ GTFABM-info/

ABOUT THE AUTHOR

Dear Readers,

Berek Morris is a native Texan, born and raised in Austin, Texas. His family consists of many authors who have inspired him to put pen to paper and to become a writer himself.

He wrote his horror anthologies, GRUESOME TALES FROM A BROKEN MIND and GRUESOME TALES FROM A BROKEN MIND #2, because he is fascinated with the human mind, the inner and outer thoughts that make us all tick. How two people can experience the same situation and walk away with two different interpretations intrigues him.

This is the second book of many. Please visit his website at http://www.berekmorris.com and sign up for his newsletter at http://www.berekmorris.com/newsletter.

Please leave a review on the retailer site where you purchased the book. You can find a link to all retailers here: http://www.berekmorris.com/GTFABM2-info

Please visit Berek Morris's website (http://www.berekmorris.com) for more information about his other novels and short stories. Feel free to contact him through his website, through his social media sites (see his website for the complete social media list) or by email at mailto: authorberekmorris@gmail.com?subject=Email% 20from%20fan.

The opinions he expresses in his stories are his own. His stories are his own intellectual property. Copyright (c) 2019,2020, Berek Morris

Sincerely,
   Berek Morris

ACKNOWLEDGMENTS

I want to give special thanks to my family for always encouraging me to be the best person I can be. I also want to thank my friends for their support.